MY FRIEND THE MONSTER

CLYDE ROBERT BULLA
MY FRIEND THE MONSTER

Illustrated by Michele Chessare

Published by The Trumpet Club
666 Fifth Avenue, New York, New York 10103

Text copyright © 1980 by Clyde Robert Bulla
Illustrations copyright © 1980 by Michele Chessare

ISBN: 0-440-84464-9

This edition published by arrangement with Harper & Row
Junior Books, a division of Harper & Row, Publishers, Inc.

Printed in the United States of America
February 1991

10 9 8 7 6 5 4 3 2 1
CW

Contents

•

1 • The Plain Prince   1

2 • The Book of Monsters   7

3 • The Dream   12

4 • Cousin Archer   16

5 • The Boy in the Woods   23

6 • Humbert's Story   29

7 • The Black Fir Twig   34

8 • "Be Ready"   40

9 • The Cages   46

10 • Beyond the Waterfall   53

11 • The Hut   59

12 • The Land Between   68

MY FRIEND
THE MONSTER

1

The Plain Prince

•

When Hal was born, people came from all over the land to see their prince and kneel by his cradle. "Oh, what a beautiful baby!" they said.

But they said it only because he was the son of the king and queen. He was not a beautiful baby, and everyone knew it—even his father and mother.

"I thought a son of ours would look quite different," said the king.

"So did I," said the queen.

"Will he ever have hair, do you think?" asked the king.

"I should think so," said the queen.

"And he will not always be so wrinkled and red?"

"I should think not," said the queen. "He may change in many ways."

So they waited, and they watched him grow. He learned to walk and talk. By that time he did have hair, and he was no longer wrinkled and red. But he was a plain child. It was clear to them that he would always be plain.

"Perhaps he will be clever," they said.

When he was old enough, he had lessons in such things as riding, music, drawing, and dancing. In not one of these did he show himself to be clever.

"Our son is not only plain," said the king, "he is ordinary."

"Yes," said the queen. "He *is* ordinary."

The boy knew they were disappointed in him, but he did not know why. He only knew that they had less and less time for him.

They gave him a room high in the castle tower. Sometimes he did not see them for weeks. Every day he sat in his window. He looked down on the court-yard at the children who played there.

He said to his father and mother, "I want to go play with them."

"That would not be right," said his father.

"Why not?" asked Hal.

"Because you are a prince and will be king one day," said his father.

"And those boys and girls are the children of servants," said his mother. "They are far beneath you."

She gave him new books and toys. He looked at the books and played with the toys while the king and queen were there. When he was alone, he looked out the window.

Sometimes the children held hands and danced in a circle. One of the girls wore a long green skirt that swirled about her. He liked to watch her. He liked it best when she left the circle and spun and whirled all by herself.

One day he saw her waving. She had seen him in the window, and she was waving to him!

He waved back.

She tilted her head to one side and pointed to his window. He was sure she was asking, "Shall I come up?"

"Yes!" he shouted, although it was too far for her to hear him. He leaned out the window and nodded his head.

In a little while he heard a tapping. He opened the door. The girl slipped into the room. She looked no older than himself, but there was paint on her face, and she wore large rings in her ears. Now he could see that her green skirt was dirty.

"It wasn't easy to get here," she told him. "The guards drove me off. They said they would break my head if they caught me again. I had to watch my chance."

She began to walk about the room, softly like a cat. Her eyes darted. She looked at his toys. She took a book off the shelf. It had a red and gold cover. "I'll trade you," she said.

Hal did not understand. "What?" he asked.

"I have a book," she said. "Will you trade it for this?"

"Yes," he said.

She looked surprised. "You will?"

"Yes, if you want me to."

She listened at the door. "Is anyone outside?"

He looked out. "There's no one."

"Then I'd better go. Don't tell anyone I was here."

She was gone. She had taken the book.

2

The Book of Monsters

.

The next day she was back. She took a book out of
the folds of her skirt.

"Here." She gave it to him. "You said you'd
trade."

The book had no cover. It was so old the pages
were yellow.

He looked into it. There were pictures on some of
the pages. They were pictures of wild-looking crea-
tures with long hair and great round eyes.

"What are they?" he asked.

"Monsters," said the girl.

The words in the book were strange to him.

"Can you read this?" he asked.

"I don't know how to read," she answered, "but I know what the book says. My mother taught me."

They sat on the floor with the book between them. "It's about the old days," she said. "The old, *old* days. Here it says there were monsters in the land. A king came to make war on them. He wanted to take their land and make slaves of them. The king's men drove them back and back until they came to Black Rock Mountain."

"I know Black Rock Mountain!" said Hal. "My Aunt Ivy lives close to it."

"The king thought he had them in a trap," said the girl, "but one of the monsters knew some magic. He made a door in the mountain. All the monsters went through, and he closed the mountain after them. There was a black square left where the door was."

"Is this a story, or is it real?" asked Hal.

"It's real."

"My teacher taught me history. Why didn't he tell me this?"

"I'll tell you why," she said. "This king was

ashamed because he was not great enough to trap a band of poor monsters. He was afraid of being laughed at. He gave out the word that no one must speak of his war with the monsters. He would not let his people write about it in any of their books."

"But someone did write about it," said Hal. "It is in this book."

"This book was made in another country," she said. "It was made in the country where my mother used to live."

She got up and began to wander about the room. Again she looked at his books and toys. Again she asked, "Is anyone outside?"

"No," he said.

"Then I must go," she said, and she was quickly gone.

The next morning the queen came up into the tower. In one hand she had the book with the red and gold cover. In the other she had a toy horse and two toy soldiers.

"Has a girl been here?" she asked.

Hal said nothing.

"You needn't answer. I know she has been." The queen's voice was cold and angry. "Yesterday the guards caught her in the tower. She had these toys hidden in her skirt. They are yours, are they not?"

"Yes," said Hal.

"The girl is a thief," said the queen. "The guards found this book in her room. She had stolen it, too."

"I gave it to her," said Hal.

"But she stole the other things," said the queen. "She had no right to come here. You should have told me."

"She meant no harm," said Hal.

"No harm? When she came here to steal from you? Well, she will give us no more trouble."

"What have you done with her?" asked Hal.

"I had her whipped," said the queen. "You shall be punished, too. I have set a guard at your door, and he will see that you have no more strange visitors."

"Mother—" began Hal.

"Hold your tongue," said the queen. "Don't think because you are a prince you can do as you please."

3

The Dream

.

Winter came, and the children no longer played in the courtyard. Hal spent more and more time with the book the girl had brought. He tried to read the words, and he looked at the pictures of the monsters. Their faces were more sad than ugly, he thought. They had become almost like friends. He gave them names. Sometimes he talked to them.

He kept the book hidden, but one day his mother saw it. He was sitting by the fire, looking at the pictures, and she was in the room before he knew she was there.

"What is this?" She took the book out of his hands. "Where did you get it?"

"It—it was here," he said.

"One of the servants must have left it," she said. "How dirty the pages are! And what ugly pictures!"

She threw it into the fireplace.

"No!" he cried.

She held him so that he could not reach the book. "Let it be," she said.

He saw that the book was in the ashes and not in the fire. He grew quiet.

She did not stay long. The moment she was gone, he ran to the fireplace. As he reached for the book, it caught fire. The pages blazed up. He thought he heard a moaning sound, as if the monsters were crying out.

That night, and for many nights afterward, Hal dreamed of monsters and fire. The dream was always the same. The monsters were holding out their hands to him. They were begging him to help them, and he could do nothing.

By the time spring came, he was thin and pale.

His mother told the king, "The prince is not well."

The king called the doctor.

The doctor looked at Hal. He told the king and queen, "This is my belief. The prince is being haunted."

"Haunted?" cried the queen.

"Yes," said the doctor. "This tower is gloomy and dark. There are ghosts that come at night to such places."

"I have not been haunted," said Hal. "No ghosts have come here."

"You would not remember." The doctor turned to the king and queen. "I should send him away for a while. I should send him to some light, bright place where no ghosts will find him."

"His Cousin Lash lives by the sea," said the king. "He could go there."

"His Aunt Ivy lives near the mountains," said the queen. "He could go there."

"And there is Lord Shanks, who lives at the edge of the forest," said the king.

"Please," said Hal, "could I choose?"

"Where do you wish to go?" asked the king.

"To my Aunt Ivy's," said Hal.

4

Cousin Archer

·

On a clear spring morning Hal set out for the country. He rode in a coach drawn by six horses. Six guards rode with him.

In the early afternoon they came to a low white house set among trees.

"You may leave me here," Hal told the guards, and they left him.

A woman came out to meet him.

"Welcome, Prince Hal." She smiled and held out her hands. "I had the queen's letter, and I have been waiting for you. I am your Aunt Ivy."

"I remember you," he said. "You came to the castle when I was little."

"I remember you, too. I'm glad you've come to stay awhile. No ghosts will find you under my roof."

"My mother says you have a son," said Hal.

"Yes. He is your Cousin Archer."

"Will he play with me?" asked Hal.

"He is not a boy," she said. "He is a man, with little time for playing. But he will welcome you when he comes home tomorrow."

She showed him his room. From his window he saw a mountain. It rose steep and dark out of the woods. He looked at it for a while.

"What do you see?" she asked.

"The mountain," he answered.

"Ah, yes, Black Rock Mountain," she said.

"There are stories about it," he said.

"Are there? What stories?"

"There is one about a door," he told her. "Not really a door, but a black square on the rock where a door used to be. I want to see it if I can."

"I know nothing of this," she said.

"It was made by magic. Monsters lived here in the

old days. They all went under the mountain, and the door closed after them. Do you know this story?"

She shook her head. "But wait—my grandmother sang a song about people who lived under the ground. And there was once a man who said he saw a monster on Black Rock Mountain."

"Do you think it was true?"

"Ask your Cousin Archer," she said. "He knows more of such things than I do."

Cousin Archer came home the next morning. He entered the room where Hal and Aunt Ivy were having breakfast. He was a big man with a black beard and round, red cheeks. His jacket and breeches were of deerskin. With one hand he led two hunting dogs. In the other he held a bag.

"Mother, I have a new bird," he said. "It is black with golden eyes."

"Archer, this is your cousin," she said. "This is Prince Hal."

"I caught the bird on its nest," said Cousin Archer. "It is alive, Mother. I can keep it with the others."

"Good day, Cousin," said Hal.

The man did not answer. He went clumping out in his heavy boots.

"My son is a great hunter," said Aunt Ivy. "He loves his birds and beasts. He has more than you can count. Go with him. He will show you."

Hal went outside. He followed a path into a garden. Cousin Archer was there. He had chained the two dogs to a tree. When they saw Hal, they began to yelp and snarl.

Cousin Archer had taken the bird out of the bag and was putting it into a cage. There were cages all along one side of the garden.

"Look," he said. "I have peacocks and pigeons and bluebirds and blackbirds. I have monkeys and foxes and tigers and bears. I have all these and many more. Have you ever seen such a sight before?"

"No," said Hal.

Cousin Archer shook the birdcages. The birds flew up and beat their wings against the bars.

"Why do you do that?" asked Hal.

Cousin Archer laughed and showed his large white teeth. "I like to see them fly!"

He went to the monkey cages. Some of the monkeys had their noses out through the bars. He struck their noses with a stick, and they chattered and screamed.

"Stop!" cried Hal.

"I like to see them make faces," said Cousin Archer.

"They make faces because you hurt them," said Hal. "Stop it."

"They are mine," said Cousin Archer. "I'll do as I like with them."

"Your mother said you loved your birds and beasts," said Hal. "If you did, you would be kind to them, and you wouldn't keep them in such cages. These cages are too small. Can't you see that?"

"You can't talk to me like this." Cousin Archer's face had grown dark and ugly. "You are only a little boy. I don't even know who you are."

Aunt Ivy had come into the garden. "This is Prince Hal," she said. "I told you that."

"I didn't hear you," he said.

"You didn't listen," she said.

"These animals are not happy," said Hal. "You should set them free."

"Set them free?" cried Cousin Archer. "I don't

care *who* you are. You can't tell me to set my animals free."

"Archer, take care," said Aunt Ivy.

"Let *him* take care. I don't believe he *is* the prince. I think he is just a little boy come to make trouble."

"Archer, you must not—" began Aunt Ivy.

But he was shouting at Hal, "Get out, or I'll set my dogs on you. Get out, and don't ever come here again!"

He was so angry his voice shook. Cutting the air with his stick, he drove Hal out of the garden.

5

The Boy in the Woods

.

Hal was more excited than afraid. He took to the road. He ran up a hill and down. When he looked back, Cousin Archer was not in sight.

Hal had come to the woods. The walk home would be easy, he thought. He had only to follow the road.

But why should he go straight home? These were the woods at the foot of Black Rock Mountain. The mountain was what he had come to see. He might climb it. He might even find where the door had been.

He walked into the deep shade. Never before had he been alone in the outdoors. Never before had he felt so free.

He came to a stream. It ran among rocks and bushes and into a pool. He lay down and drank from the pool.

As he got to his feet, he saw a heap of clothing under the bushes beside him. There were breeches and a pair of boots. There was a coat. There was a shirt. On top of the heap was a little cap.

Hal picked up the boots. They were thick and heavy. He picked up the breeches, the coat, the shirt. They were made of rough brown cloth such as he had never seen before.

He tried on the cap. There were two holes in it— one on either side.

He wondered who had worn such things. He wondered why they were here. He looked at them for a little while. Then he put them down and went on toward the mountain.

Before he had gone far, he heard steps behind him. He turned. A boy was running after him. He wore the clothes Hal had found under the bush.

Strange sounds came from the boy's wide-open mouth.

For a moment Hal stopped breathing. The boy was a monster.

He had a monster face with great round eyes and a flat nose. His teeth were tusks. His hair was like a lion's mane. His skin was green. A pair of pink horns showed through the holes in his cap.

"Give it back!" he shouted in a small, furry voice.

He threw himself upon Hal. Hal felt the monster's claws dig into his arm.

The monster was strong, but he was awkward. Hal quickly pushed him to the ground and held him there.

The monster boy stopped fighting. He looked up into Hal's face. "Give it back," he said. "It's nothing to you. *Give it back to me!*"

"Give *what* back?" asked Hal.

"The twig!" said the monster boy.

"I don't know what you mean," said Hal.

"You do. You know you do. You found my clothes. I was across the pool—I saw you. You took the twig."

"I didn't take anything," said Hal.

"You did. It was in my cap. Give it to me!"

"I tell you, I don't have it," said Hal.

The monster boy lay still. Tears ran down his cheeks. "What shall I do?" he said.

Hal stood up. Still the monster boy lay there.

"What was the twig you lost?" asked Hal. "I'll help you find it."

"You would never help me," said the monster boy. "You are a Small-Eyes."

"A what?"

"A Small-Eyes," said the monster boy. "We people under the mountain have eyes like mine. But you have small eyes, and you hate us."

"How could I hate you? I don't even know you." Hal was staring at the boy—at his tusks, his long hair, his green skin. "Are you really from under the mountain?"

"Yes," said the monster boy, "and without the twig I can never go home again. The Small-Eyes will find me and kill me."

"Why can't you go home without the twig?" asked Hal.

Something moved in the bushes beside them.

The monster boy started to his feet. "What was that?"

"Only a bird," said Hal. "See? There it goes."

But there was still fright in the monster's eyes. "I must not stay here," he said. "Someone will be coming by."

Hal looked about him. He saw a great clump of ferns. "These will hide us," he said.

They pushed their way into the ferns. They made a kind of nest and sat there. Now the monster's face was not so wild and full of fear. There was something almost gentle in his eyes.

"I didn't take the twig. I didn't take anything from you," said Hal. "Won't you believe me?"

"Yes, I believe you now," said the monster boy.

"What *is* the twig?" asked Hal. "Who are you? How did you get here?"

The monster boy dried his eyes. Slowly and softly he began to talk.

6

Humbert's Story

.

"My name is Humbert," he said. "I was born in the land under the mountain. My father knew magic. The magic came down through our family from the old days. Just before he died, he told me there was a way out of our land. It was a secret he had kept, and no one else knew it."

Hal had to listen closely. The words in the boy's soft, furry voice were hard to understand.

Humbert went on, "He kept it a secret because of the danger in the world above. If we went there and the Small-Eyes found us, they would do us harm.

This is what he told me. Yet he wanted me to see the world above."

"Why," asked Hal, "if he thought there was danger?"

"Because it was so beautiful," said Humbert. "He wanted me to see the sun and sky, the trees and grass. He said he would take me when I was older. But then he fell ill, and I knew he could never take me. I asked for the secret, so I could go alone. Before he gave it to me, I had to make two promises. I promised to give the secret to no one in our land. And I promised to take only one look at the world above. I broke that promise. Now I can never go home."

"Why?" asked Hal.

"Because of the twig," answered Humbert. "It was from a black fir tree. It was old and dry—only a little stick. It came from the world above. There was not another in our land. When I touched the door with it and spoke the magic words, the mountain opened and let me through."

"I have heard of this door," said Hal.

"I wish I had never heard of it," said Humbert. "When I saw the world above, one look was not enough. I came for another and another. I saw no one, and I forgot the danger. Today I swam in the pool. Then I saw you. I hid in the bushes and watched you. And now the twig is gone."

"It may not be," said Hal. "Shall we try to find it?"

"I have already tried," said Humbert.

"Shall we try again?"

They went back to the pool. They looked under the bushes and among the rocks. They even looked under the sticks and leaves.

"You see," said Humbert. "It is not here. I wore it in my cap, and—"

"It must have fallen into the pool when I picked up your cap," said Hal.

They looked down at the water.

"If it fell into the pool, we can never find it," said Humbert.

"And I am to blame," said Hal.

Humbert shook his head. "I am to blame—because I came here."

They sat by the pool.

"Must it be this one twig?" asked Hal. "Would another do as well?"

"It must be a black fir twig," said Humbert.

"I know where there is a black fir tree," said Hal.

Humbert sat up straight. "You do?"

"Yes," said Hal. "In our garden at home."

Humbert asked quickly, "Is it far?"

"Half a day from here," answered Hal. "If we take the road, we can— No. Someone would see us."

"And I think most Small-Eyes are not like you," said Humbert. "They would do me harm. No. I must not go with you."

"Then I'll go alone," said Hal.

"You would do this for me?"

"Yes," said Hal. "But you will have a long time to wait. You may be hungry before I come back."

"There are roots to eat."

They went back to the clump of ferns. "You can hide here while I am gone," said Hal.

Humbert asked, "What is your name?"

"Hal."

"What does it mean?"

"I don't know."

"I think it means 'someone good,' " said Humbert.

7

The Black Fir Twig

Hal took the road toward home. People came out of their houses to look at him. He wondered why, until he heard a woman say, "See the clothes he wears!"

His clothes were of silk and velvet. Perhaps it was odd, he thought, to see a boy dressed like a king's son walking alone on the road.

Under a bridge he took off his clothes. He turned them inside out and put them on again. He tore them here and there to make them look ragged. He put dirt on his face. Now he looked like a beggar.

He went on until he came to a village. In a shop

window he saw cakes and bread and cheese. He went into the shop.

"I'd like some bread and cheese," he told the woman there.

"Let me see your money," she said.

"I have none."

"Be off with you." She had a broom in her hands, and she swept him out of the shop.

Not until then had he ever thought of money. He had never needed any before.

He remembered that the buttons on his coat were gold. He pulled one of them off and went back into the shop.

"Will you take this for money?"

"Where did you steal this?" asked the woman. But she took it and gave him bread and a piece of cheese. He stood outside and ate them. Nothing had ever tasted so good to him before.

He left the village. He thought of Humbert waiting alone, and he walked faster.

At sunset he came to the castle. His father and mother must not see him, he told himself. They would ask a hundred questions. He might be shut up in the tower. If he hoped to take Humbert a twig from the black fir tree, he must come and go in secret.

The castle gates were closed for the night. Beggars were sitting against the walls. Hal sat down among them. No one spoke to him. A baby was crying, and a woman sang very softly. The song put Hal to sleep.

In the morning the beggars gathered at the front gate. Hal was with them. He hoped that when the gate opened he might slip through.

Some of the beggars were looking at him. "Who are you?" asked one. "We never saw you before."

"Go and beg somewhere else," said another. "This place is for us."

Hal went to the back gate. It was open.

He put more dirt on his face and pulled his hair down over his eyes. He looked through the gate.

"Ho, dirty-face," said the guard. "What do you want?"

"They say the king's garden is a wonderful sight," said Hal. "I want to see it."

"Be off," said the man.

"Will you let me in for this?" Hal held up another of his gold buttons.

"Something you've stolen, no doubt." But the guard took the button. "Come and have a look—but be quick."

Hal went into the garden. He found the black fir tree, small and dark against the wall. When he thought the guard was not looking, he broke off a twig.

But the guard had seen him. "You dog!" he shouted. "I said you might look, not break pieces off the trees!"

Hal dodged past the man and out through the gate. He ran. The guard threw sticks and called him ugly names, but Hal did not care. The black fir twig was safe inside his clothes.

He walked back the way he had come. The sun was high when he came to the woods at the foot of Black Rock Mountain.

He went straight to the clump of ferns. "Humbert!" he called in a low voice.

There was no answer.

"Humbert!" he called a little louder. "It's Hal."

As he spoke, he knew that something was wrong. Some of the ferns lay flat. Some were broken and torn up by the roots.

He pushed his way into the clump. He came to the nest he and Humbert had made. Humbert was gone.

8

"Be Ready"

.

All the rest of the day Hal looked for Humbert. He looked by the pool and among the trees. He called, "Humbert, where are you?"

When night came he slept in the ferns. In the morning he was hungry. He remembered what Humbert had said about finding roots to eat.

He dug up a few roots. He washed them in the pool and ate them. They were bitter and tough. He drank some water. Still the bitter taste was in his mouth, but he was no longer hungry.

He went back to his search. "Humbert!" he called.

Near the road he stopped at the sound of voices. While he listened, people came in sight—a crowd of men, women, and children. They were coming down the road toward him.

"You, there!" called a man. "Can you tell us where to find Archer the hunter?"

Hal pointed. "That way."

"Have you been there?" asked the man. "Have you seen it?"

"Seen what?" asked Hal.

"The monster," said the man.

Hal stared at him.

"Don't you know about the monster?" asked the man. "The hunter caught it in the woods."

"When?" asked Hal.

"Yesterday, I think," said the man.

"Did he—did he harm it?" asked Hal.

"Harm it?" said the man. "*I* don't know."

The people moved on. Hal went with them.

"That must be the house," said a woman.

"Yes," said a man. "I see the hunter."

Cousin Archer was out in front of the house. He looked pleased and important.

"I know why you are here," he said. "You have come to see my prize."

"Yes!" cried the people.

"Oh, he's an ugly one," said Cousin Archer. "He put up a fight, I can tell you, but my dogs and I soon took care of him."

"Show us the monster!" cried the people.

"Very well," said Cousin Archer, "but only for a little while. Others will be waiting. They have been coming here all morning."

He led the people into the garden. Hal kept to the middle of the crowd where Cousin Archer could not see him.

Someone said, "There it is—in the cage!"

Hal pushed forward with the others. He looked into the cage. Humbert was there, curled up with his hands over his face.

"Let me tell you how it was," said Cousin Archer. "I was hunting, and I came to a clump of ferns. When the ferns moved, I knew something was hiding in them. My dogs knew it, too. I sent them in. They caught this fine fellow and dragged him out."

"The monster wears clothes!" someone said.

"Yes. He even had a cap, but that was lost." Cousin Archer reached into the cage and poked Humbert with a stick. "Show your face, you ugly brute!"

Humbert looked out with his great wild eyes. He spoke.

"The monster is talking!" cried a woman.

"No, no. Sometimes he makes sounds that are a little like words," said Cousin Archer, "but they make no sense. He is only a monster."

But Hal had caught the words in Humbert's thick, strange voice. He had said, "Don't hurt me."

A man asked, "What will you do with the monster?"

"Keep it with my other animals," said Cousin Archer.

"Ah, but this one is different," said the man. "You could put him in a show. People would pay to see such a creature."

"That they would," said another man. "The monster is worth a fortune."

Cousin Archer told the crowd, "You have seen enough. Others are waiting to come in."

The people would not go.

"Look at his long teeth," someone said. "See how the horns come out of his head."

"You must go, all of you." Cousin Archer was growing angry. He tried to push them out. The dogs barked. They were chained to a tree, and they threw themselves forward as far as they could go. Slowly the people began to leave.

Hal hung back.

"Humbert," he said.

The boy in the cage gave a start. He looked out through the bars. "Hal!" he said.

"I have the twig," said Hal. "Be ready."

And while Cousin Archer was driving people out of the garden, Hal climbed into a tree and hid himself in the thick branches.

9

The Cages

•

While the day went by, Hal sat in the tree. He peeped through the leaves at the people who came and went. He grew tired. He grew hungry and thirsty.

At sundown Cousin Archer sent the last of the crowds away. The gates were closed for the night.

Still there were voices below. Hal looked down. In the shadows he could see Cousin Archer with three of his servants.

"You will stand guard tonight," Cousin Archer was saying. "The monster is worth a fortune. Someone may try to break in and carry him off."

He went away.

Hal watched the garden grow dark. He tried to think what to do. His plan had been to wait until Humbert was left alone. Then he would climb down and set him free. But now the three men were there, standing guard in front of the cage.

Birds in the cages made sleepy, clucking sounds. As Hal listened, an idea came to him.

He knew where all the cages were. Humbert's was alone in the middle of the garden. The others were on the far side. He was sure he could find them all, even in the dark.

Very quietly he climbed down out of the tree. He felt his way to where the birds were. He found a cage door and slid it open.

He had thought the birds would come flying out, but they hardly moved.

He went on to the monkeys. He opened one cage, then another and another. Like the birds, the monkeys hardly moved. They were asleep, he thought.

He reached into a cage. He touched a monkey's tail. The monkey gave a scream.

In a moment the others began to chatter and scream. He heard them scampering out of their cages.

He threw open more cages. The birds squawked. Cousin Archer's dogs were barking.

Now the men were shouting. "What's that?" "The monkeys are out!" "Catch them!" "Go for a light!"

They had left their place in front of Humbert's cage. While they were running about the garden, Hal went to the cage and opened it.

"It's Hal," he whispered, and Humbert was beside him.

"This way," said Hal, and they started off together.

Out of the dark something leaped against Hal. Something tore at his shoulder. He fell backward and was free.

"Quick," he said. "Up the tree."

He climbed the tree that grew close to the garden wall. He stepped out on top of the wall. Humbert was behind him.

Hal jumped. Humbert jumped after him. They bumped into each other as they rolled down a hill.

Hal held on to Humbert's arm. Humbert was trembling.

"What shall we do?" he asked.

"We'll go to the mountain," said Hal.

"The mountain, yes!" said Humbert.

They ran through the darkness. They ran until the shouts and screams in the garden were far behind.

They came to the road. Ahead of them the sky was bright.

"What is the light?" asked Humbert.

"The moon is coming up," answered Hal. "It will help us see the way."

But it would help Cousin Archer, too, if he followed them.

Hal stopped to feel his shoulder.

"Are you hurt?" asked Humbert.

"A dog bit me," said Hal.

"Shall we stop?" asked Humbert.

"No," said Hal.

Humbert asked, "Where is the twig?"

"Inside my shirt."

"Is it a black fir twig? Are you sure?"

"It's from the tree in the castle garden. My father called it a black fir."

They left the road. They were running through the woods. The moon rose, and light shone down through the trees.

Hal heard the barking of dogs.

Humbert heard it, too. "Are they after us?"

"I think so. I think they are on our trail." Hal's shoulder had begun to sting and burn. He felt dizzy.

They were near the foot of the mountain. Now Humbert led the way.

The dogs were closer. Their barking had changed to a kind of cry. Once Hal heard another sound. He was sure it was Cousin Archer's voice.

Humbert had stopped.

"Run!" said Hal.

"No. Wait. Here it is." Humbert stood before a wall of rock. "Give me the twig."

Hal gave it to him. Humbert held it against the wall. He spoke a few words.

There was a deep rumble. A door opened in the rock.

Humbert pushed Hal through. He spoke again, and the door closed after them.

10

Beyond the Waterfall

•

Hal and Humbert stood side by side in a soft green brightness. Overhead was a swarm of lights like tiny green stars.

Hal looked back at the door that had closed and shut out Cousin Archer and his dogs. It was a dark square on a wall of rock.

"Don't be afraid," said Humbert. "This is The Land Between."

"What is The Land Between?" asked Hal.

"The land between my world and yours."

"Aren't we—aren't we under the mountain?" asked Hal.

"Yes," answered Humbert.

"But how can we see stars under the mountain?"

"They are not stars. My people say they are ghost-lights, and they are afraid to come here. But the lights are only from glowworms that come out on the rocks. My father told me so."

"Glowworms!" said Hal. "I've seen them at home, but never so many."

He tried to look at his shoulder. His coat was torn and bloody. His arm was numb, and he could no longer lift it.

"I forgot!" said Humbert. "You are hurt. Come."

"Where?"

"To my mother. She can make you well."

"Is it far?"

"We can rest on the way," said Humbert.

They walked in the dry bed of a river. Hal could feel sand and small rocks under his feet.

They came to a waterfall. It fell from high above like a wide curtain and swept away in a swift stream.

Humbert waded into the water. "Follow me. It isn't deep."

The water came only to the tops of Humbert's boots. He disappeared behind the waterfall.

Hal followed. All was dark behind the waterfall, and the water roared in his ears. He pushed one foot before the other until he came out on the other side. Humbert was waiting there.

Beyond the waterfall, the land was different. There were no glowworms, yet there was light. It showed red on the rocks overhead. It flickered and was never still.

They were climbing. For Hal the climb was steep and slow.

He looked down from the top of a hill. It was like looking into a great cave, a great hollow under the mountain. And now he knew why the light was red, why it flickered. It was firelight. As far as he could see, across the floor of the land, there were fires. Some leaped high. Others burned low. The air was thick with smoke.

"Is all the land on fire?" asked Hal.

Humbert told him, "There is a kind of rock that we dig out of the ground. It burns, and we keep fires going."

"Why?" asked Hal.

"The fires give us light," said Humbert, "and my people believe fire keeps away the ghosts that live under the mountain."

They rested on the hilltop. There was a path ahead. It wound among rocks that stood like tall men.

Hal felt weak and ill.

"I can't go any farther," he said.

"Wait. I'll bring my mother." Humbert ran off down the path.

Hal lay on the ground and closed his eyes. He was falling asleep. . . .

The sound of footsteps wakened him. He heard a woman say in a thick, hoarse voice, "But he is a Small-Eyes! Why have you brought him here? What shall we do?"

"He is hurt," said Humbert.

"Yes, I see. He has lost blood," said the woman.

"But we dare not take him home. He is our enemy. If someone sees us—"

"He is not our enemy," said Humbert. "Lift him—there! I'll walk close to you. If we hide his face, no one will know."

Hal felt himself being carried, and he was not sure whether he was dreaming or awake.

11
The Hut

•

There were times of half-sleeping and half-waking. There were times of pain. Hal saw lights, he heard voices. None of them seemed real.

A time came when there was no more pain. He knew where he was and how he had got there. He was on a bed in a small stone hut. Beside him was a lamp that burned with a smoky light.

This was Humbert's hut in the land under Black Rock Mountain. Humbert's mother had carried him there.

The hut had high walls but no roof. There was no need for one, he thought. Under the mountain the weather must always be the same, with no sunshine or rain.

Humbert and his mother were near. He could hear them talking.

"Can't you make him well?" asked Humbert.

"I have done all I can," said the woman. "Why do you care so much?"

"I told you, he saved me," said Humbert. "He is my friend."

"Why won't you listen to me?" said his mother. "You are only a monster to this Small-Eyes. Do you think he would ever say of you, 'This is my friend the monster'?"

Hal moved his head until he could see the woman. She was sitting across the room from him. She had round, red eyes and a flat nose like a pig's. Her teeth were tusks. Her dress was made of stuff like sackcloth. She picked at it with her long, sharp claws.

Humbert sat on the floor beside her. He said, "No matter what you say, he is my friend."

"You don't understand these things." The woman began to weep. "This Small-Eyes is our enemy. If anyone else knew he was here, we would be in danger."

"No one else knows," said Humbert.

"I think someone saw us bring him here," she said. "The neighbors are whispering. Haven't you seen them at the door, trying to peep in?"

"Be quiet," said Humbert. "He is awake."

He came to the bed.

"Humbert—" said Hal.

"Now you know my name!" said Humbert. "You are better!"

His mother came and looked down at Hal.

"You carried me here," said Hal. "I remember that."

"I did it for my son," she said.

"Thank you," said Hal. "If you hadn't cared for me—"

She turned away.

Humbert brought a bowl of food. "Can you eat?"

The food was lumpy and gray. It looked like paste.

"What is it?" asked Hal.

"It is what we've been giving you," Humbert told him. "There are mushrooms in it. There is fish—"

His mother said, "I hear someone." She looked out, and Hal heard her say, "No, you can't come in. No, there is no trouble."

She closed the door.

"Who was it?" asked Humbert.

"I don't know," she said. "I never saw him before. He asked if there was trouble here."

"Am I the trouble?" asked Hal.

"Yes, you are," she said.

"Then I must go," said Hal.

But when he tried to get up, he could not stand.

More time passed—how much, Hal did not know. Under the mountain there were no days. All was night.

He grew stronger. He began to walk about the hut.

Children came to the door. He heard their sing-song voices.

"Who's there?" they called. "Who's there, who's there?"

Humbert's mother called back, "*I* am here."

"Who else?" they asked. "Who else—who else?"

"My son," she answered.

"Let us see," they called. "Why will you let no one see?"

"Be off with you!" she said.

Hal was sitting on the bed. He looked up as a stone fell from above.

More stones came in over the walls of the hut. They began to fall like hail.

Humbert's mother ran out. There were screams, then all was still.

She came back in. She was out of breath. "I knocked their heads together. They won't come here again."

"They *will* come," said Humbert.

They looked at Hal.

"I'll go," he said.

"Yes, go now," said the woman. "Go while there is no one outside."

"Good-bye," he said, "and thank you."

"Never mind that," she said.

Hal and Humbert left the hut. They ran through the firelight.

Halfway up the hill, Humbert said, "They're coming after us."

"I don't see anyone," said Hal.

"I can hear them."

"What if they catch us?" asked Hal.

"They have never seen anyone like you here," said Humbert. "They might—" He stopped.

"What?" asked Hal.

"They might not let you go." Humbert asked, "Do you know how to get back to the door in the mountain?"

"I don't know," said Hal.

"Back of the waterfall to The Land Between," said Humbert. "Follow the riverbed to the door."

"Yes," said Hal. "I think I remember."

"Go on alone," said Humbert. "I'll stay here. If they come up the path, I'll stop them."

"By yourself?"

"Yes." Humbert put his hand on one of the tall

stones. "I'll push this down the path." He asked, "Can you find the door without me?"

"I think so," said Hal, "but—"

"Here." Humbert put something into Hal's hand. It was the black fir twig. "This is what to say to open the door." He told Hal the words. "Now go. Run!"

Hal ran until he came to the waterfall. He felt his way through the darkness behind it.

In the green light of The Land Between, he followed the riverbed. A black square showed on a rocky wall ahead—the door in the mountain.

He took the twig out of his shirt. He touched the door with it.

What were the words Humbert had told him?

"Black fir—"

No.

He closed his eyes and tried again. The words came slowly:

"Fir black
Trik-trak—
Open!"

There was a deep rumbling sound. The door opened. He went through. He said:

"Fir black
Trik-trak—
Close!"

The door closed. He was outside the mountain, in sunlight so bright that for a little while he could hardly see.

12

The Land Between

·

Hal walked to the road. While he rested there, two of the king's guards rode by and found him.

They leaped off their horses and knelt before him.

"These many days we have looked for you!" cried one.

"Everyone in the land has looked!" cried the other. "Please speak to us and tell us you are well."

"I am well enough, but a little tired," said Hal. "I'll be glad of a ride."

One of the guards gave him a ride home.

There was great excitement in the castle. The

queen wept when she saw the prince in his torn clothes. The king asked over and over, "Where have you been? *Where?*"

"I was in the woods—" began Hal.

"All these days and nights?" asked the king. "Where did you go when you disappeared from your Aunt Ivy's?"

"I didn't disappear," said Hal. "I was made to go."

"We know," said the king, "and your Cousin Archer has been punished. All his birds and beasts have been set free, and he has been sent away for a year. . . . But where did you go?"

Hal began again, "I was in the woods—"

"Did you know your Cousin Archer found a monster in the woods?" asked the king. "It ran away in the night. We feared that you had met this terrible creature."

"We feared it had carried you off," said the queen.

"Nothing carried me off," said Hal.

"Then what happened?" asked the king. "Tell us!"

"Stop asking him questions," said the queen. "Can't you see he needs rest and care?"

She and the king went with him to his room in the tower. The queen put him to bed. When no one was looking, he took the black fir twig out from under his shirt and hid it in the bedclothes.

The doctor came.

The queen had taken off Hal's ragged coat and shirt.

"Ah!" said the doctor.

"What is it?" asked the king.

"All is clear to me," said the doctor. "The prince has been under a spell."

The queen turned pale. The king asked, "What kind of spell?"

"The spell of the Witch of the Woods," said the doctor. "She has met the prince, and—"

"I saw no Witch of the Woods," said Hal.

"You would not remember, but you did meet her. How do I know? I'll tell you. She has put her sign on you." The doctor pointed to Hal's shoulder.

The queen began to weep.

"You must not weep," said the doctor. "This is most wonderful. The Witch of the Woods has marked him with her sign of the rose. And whoever is marked with her sign will be wise and good forever after."

"Wise and good?" said the king. He and the queen looked at each other. They looked at Hal almost as if they had never seen him before.

"My dear son," said the queen, "you *have* changed. I can see it in your face."

Hal wanted to say, "How can you believe such foolishness? I am just as I was before, except for the mark on my shoulder where Cousin Archer's dog bit me."

But he was quiet. The questions had stopped, and he was glad. He had kept Humbert's secret.

Hal slept and ate. He grew strong again. One day he told his mother, "I want to go away for a while."

"Where?" she asked.

"To Black Rock Mountain," he said.

"Ah, you wish to visit your Aunt Ivy," said the queen. "That is a kind thought. With her son gone, she must be lonely."

Six guards took Hal away in a coach. Near Black Rock Mountain he said, "You may put me down here."

The guards put him down, and he struck out through the woods. He walked to the foot of the mountain.

He found the black square in the wall. He took the twig out of his shirt, touched it to the stone, and spoke the words:

"Fir black
Trik-trak—
Open!"

The door opened. He went through.
He said:

"Fir black
Trik-trak—
Close!"

The door closed. He was under the mountain. And there before him, in the strange green light, was Humbert.

His great eyes were bright. He said, "I've been waiting."

"I wanted to come before," Hal said. "I was afraid harm had come to you because of me."

"No harm," said Humbert. "After you left me, some men came up the hill to where I was. When they saw I was alone, they went away."

"Humbert—" began Hal.

There was something he wanted to say. He had the words ready:

I am a prince. Someday I'll be king. Then you and your people may come out from under the mountain and no one will harm you.

But he waited. It might be too much for Humbert to believe all at once. Or it might make a difference between them. Humbert might kneel before him . . .

It must be told carefully, he thought, a little at a time.

He said instead, "I saw no one as I came through the woods. Shall we walk outside?"

"Sometime, if you like, but not now," answered Humbert. "There is no danger to you here, and none to me, and the glowworms are bright."

So they walked down the old riverbed. It made a smooth road. They came to the waterfall and sat for a while before it.

"Do you know games?" asked Hal.

"I know some," said Humbert.

"Will you teach me?" asked Hal.

"Yes," said Humbert.

"I want to learn them when I come again," said Hal. "Now I must go to my Aunt Ivy's."

"When will you come again?" asked Humbert.

"Tomorrow," Hal told him.

And the next day and many days after that the two friends met. They played games, they walked and talked, sometimes they were happy just to be quiet together, and The Land Between was theirs alone.

About the Author

CLYDE ROBERT BULLA is one of America's best-known writers for young people. The broad scope of his interests has led him to write more than fifty distinguished books on a variety of subjects, including travel, history, science, and music. He has received a number of awards for his contributions to the field of children's books, including, for *Shoeshine Girl*, awards in three states—Oklahoma, Arkansas, and South Carolina—the winners of which were voted upon by school children.

Clyde Bulla's early years were spent on a farm near King City, Missouri. He now lives and works in the bustling city of Los Angeles. When he is not busy writing a book, he loves to travel.